PUFFIN BOOKS

Treasure Trove

Dick King-Smith served in the Grenadier Guards
during the Second World War, and afterwards
spent twenty years as a farmer in Gloucestershire,
the county of his birth. Many of his stories are
inspired by his farming experiences. Later he
taught at a village primary school. His first book,
The Fox Busters, was published in 1978. Since then
he has written a great number of children's books,
including *The Sheep-Pig* (winner of the *Guardian*
Award and filmed as *Babe*), *Harry's Mad*, *Noah's
Brother*, *The Hodgeheg*, *Martin's Mice*, *Ace*, *The Cuckoo
Child* and *Harriet's Hare* (winner of the Children's
Book Award in 1995). At the British Book Awards
in 1992 he was voted Children's Author of the
Year. He is married, with three children and
elevengrandchildren, and lives in a seventeenth-
century cottage a short crow's-flight from the house
where he was born.

Dick King-Smith

Treasure Trove

Illustrated by Paul Howard

PUFFIN BOOKS

PUFFIN BOOKS

Published by the Penguin Group
Penguin Books Ltd, 27 Wrights Lane, London W8 5TZ, England
Penguin Putnam Inc., 375 Hudson Street, New York,
New York 10014, USA
Penguin Books Australia Ltd, Ringwood, Victoria, Australia
Penguin Books Canada Ltd, 10 Alcorn Avenue, Toronto, Ontario,
Canada M4V 3B2
Penguin Books (NZ) Ltd, Cnr Rosedale and Airborne Roads, Albany,
Auckland, New Zealand

Penguin Books Ltd, Registered Offices: Harmondsworth,
Middlesex, England

First published by Viking 1996
Published in Puffin Books 1998
7 9 10 8 6

Made and printed in England by Clays Ltd, St Ives plc

British Library Cataloguing in Publication Data
A CIP catalogue record for this book is available from the British Library

ISBN 0–140–38013–2

Contents

CHAPTER 1

THE SQUEAKY
FLOORBOARD

Just outside Ben's bedroom door there was a floorboard that squeaked, as though it was protesting at being trodden on.

Ben had been going along this landing on his way to or from his bedroom ever since he could walk – for about seven years. Every time he trod on this section of floorboard, a piece about two and a half feet by a foot, it squeaked at him.

This had happened thousands of times, and it had never occurred to Ben to wonder why, because he was so used to the squeak.

Until one morning, as he was coming out of his room, he took some coins out of the pocket of his jeans, to count how much money he had, and dropped one of the smallest, a 5p piece. It rolled along the floor and before Ben could stop it, it dropped neatly through the thinnest of cracks between the noisy floorboard and its neighbour.

5p may not be much to some people, but it was a lot to Ben. Not that he was specially mean, but he was very interested in money. It was important to him. Saving was a form of collecting for him. Others might collect stamps or empty crisp-packets or fossils. With Ben, it was money.

He had a proper little steel cash-box which he had been given as a Christmas present, with two keys (in case you lost one). Inside, there was a black plastic tray divided into four equal-sized compartments. In these he kept four different kinds of coins – £1, 50p, 20p and 10p. Anything smaller – 5p, 2p or 1p pieces – he kept in his pocket and thought of them as his pocket-money.

These he could spend. The rest he saved.

For some time the going rate from his father had been £1 per week, but on Ben's eighth birthday he had asked for a rise.

'Why?' his father said. 'You'll only waste it if I give you more.'

'No, I won't,' said Ben. 'I'm saving a fraction of everything I get.'

'A fraction, eh? You know about them, do you?'

'Yes, we're doing them in maths.'

'So what fraction are you saving?' his father asked.

'Well, I don't know exactly,' Ben said. 'You see, I only spend the small coins – 5ps, 2ps and pennies.'

'Then you must be saving quite a bit.'

'Yes. But I could save more if you gave me more. You're lucky really, Dad, you know.'

'Why?'

'Because I'm an only child. Suppose I had had a brother or sister, you'd be forking out £2 a week instead of £1. That's twice as much.'

'You're asking me for £2 a week?'

'No. Though it could come to that. It depends.'

'Depends on what?'

'How much small change you've got in your pocket at the end of each day. 5p pieces or smaller, I mean. If you put those aside every day, you could give me the lot at the end of the week, on top of my usual £1. It might not

4

be much or it might be quite a lot. It's a gamble, you see, Dad. How about it?'

Ben's father grinned at him.

'You're a cunning monkey,' he said. 'Because the idea's quite attractive, I must say. All those pennies and 2p pieces are a nuisance in my pocket, I find, and especially those horrible little 5ps.'

'So will you?'

'OK. I'll risk it.'

On this particular morning it was one of those 'horrible little 5ps' that had disappeared down the crack in the floorboards.

Since his new scheme for extra pocket money had started, Ben had had a couple of good weeks. At the end of the first week, his father had handed over 73p in small change on top of the usual £1, and the second week brought in 59p.

But this, the third week, had produced only 24p – seven 2ps, five pennies, and just the one 5p piece, so that Ben was not at all happy about losing it.

Only one way to get it back, he thought. I'll have to take that squeaky floorboard up. It must be a bit loose anyway, I suppose – that's why it squeaks.

Ben had a good look at the floorboard. He imagined that he'd have to borrow some of his father's tools, on the quiet, so that he could get the nails out and then get the board up. But when he went down on his hands and knees to have a closer look, he could see that at either

end there were nail-holes but no nails in them. Someone, it seemed, must have had that board up before, for some reason.

Ben opened the big blade of his Swiss Army knife. He slipped it into the crack down which the coin had dropped, and found that he could lever up the short section of floorboard as easy as winking.

He peered into the space below. In between the joists, a lot of fluff and dust and stuff had collected, and, sifting through this with his fingers, he found the runaway 5p piece.

He put it in his pocket and was about to replace the floorboard, when it occurred to him to wonder just why it had not been fastened down. That was the reason it squeaked, of course – it wasn't nailed tight, so it moved a little underfoot.

Someone must once have drawn those nails so that it could be easily raised and replaced. But why? Could it perhaps have been some child's hiding-place for something, years ago? The cottage was very old – at least three hundred years old, he knew – so a lot of children must have lived in it, over the centuries.

Ben began to feel under the boards on either side, reaching as far as he could into the six spaces between the three joists that ran across. From five he pulled nothing but more fluff and dust and bits of plaster but in the sixth space his fingers touched something.

His finger-tips told him that it was some sort of bag, containing something hard.

Ben lay down on his side, his shoulder in the hole, and with a mighty effort managed to grab hold of the bag. It was heavy, he felt as he straightened up, and it was made, he could now see, of stout canvas, its mouth closed by a

drawstring. Whatever was in it made a clinking, chinking sound.

Just then he heard the door open at the bottom of the cottage's narrow curving little staircase and then his mother's footstep on the bottom step.

Quick as a flash, he set the floorboard back in place, and, bag in hand, nipped into the bathroom and locked the door.

'Ben! Where are you?' he heard his mother call.

'In the loo,' he said.

'OK. Don't be long. Breakfast's ready.'

Ben waited till he heard the stairs door close again, and then he sat on the turned-down lid of the loo, and pulled open the drawstring of the canvas bag.

Inside was a mass of gold coins.

CHAPTER 2

A BIT OF DIY

The space beneath the squeaky floorboard had not been a child's hiding-place then! No child would have owned gold coins like those, or so many of them. They must be the life savings of someone who lived here in this cottage long ago, lived in my own bedroom probably, Ben thought, and then died without ever spending that money, about which no one else could have known.

What were these coins? How many of them were there? What would they be worth?

Then he heard his mother's voice again.

'Hurry up, Ben. You'll be late for school at this rate.'

Hastily Ben pulled the drawstring of the

canvas bag tight again. He flushed the loo, to make it sound as if he'd been using it, and unlocked the bathroom door. Quickly he levered up the squeaky floorboard again with his knife, dropped in the bag, and replaced the board. Then he tore downstairs.

'Sorry I'm late,' he said, helping himself to cornflakes, a big smile on his face at the thought of that hidden treasure.

'You don't look exactly sorry about anything,' his mother said. 'What are you so pleased about?'

'Oh, nothing.'

'He looks as though he'd lost a penny and found a shilling,' his father said.

'There aren't shillings any more, Dad,' Ben said.

'More's the pity. Coins used to be much more interesting – farthings, threepenny bits, florins, half-crowns, sovereigns. Lovely names that all disappeared when we went decimal.'

'When was that, Dad?'

'1971, I think it was. I was about your age.'

'Were any of those gold?'

'Sovereigns, yes. A couple of hundred years before that there were all sorts of different gold coins. They'd be very valuable nowadays, I imagine.'

'What, if someone found one, you mean?' said Ben.

'Stop chattering and eat your breakfast, do, Ben,' said his mother. 'I've never known anyone talk about money as much as you do.'

'He's quite the businessman,' her husband said. 'Conned me into a scheme for giving him more pocket money. He'll end up as rich as Croesus, I shouldn't wonder.'

'Who was Croesus?'

'An old king who had masses of money.'

'Ben, *will* you eat up?' said his mother.

'I might,' Ben said.

'No "might" about it, you will! Just do as you're told.'

'No,' said Ben. 'I mean I might end up as rich as Croesus.'

At school that day the time dragged by. Ben was longing to be home again, to take up that floorboard once more.

He tried to remember the look of the coins but couldn't. He sat in a dream, not listening to his teacher, writing a story that was rubbish, getting many of his sums wrong, and, after lunch, which he hardly tasted, continually looking at the time by the classroom clock.

At last his teacher could bear it no longer.

'Ben!' she said.

'Yes, Miss?'

'School ends at 3.15.'

'Yes, Miss, I know.'

'That is not for another hour.'

'No, Miss, I know.'

'Then stop looking at the clock and do some work!'

'Yes, Miss.'

Ben rested his left arm across his desk as he wrote so that he could see his watch, and never did time go so slowly.

But by the time the bell rang for the end of school, he had not entirely wasted the day. He had made up his mind about one thing. I'm not going to tell Mum and Dad about the gold, he said to himself. I found it, so it's finders keepers.

At home again, he dashed upstairs.

'You're in a hurry,' his mother called after him.

'Going to do my homework,' Ben shouted back.

'Well, answer the phone if it rings,' his mother said. 'I'm going out in the garden to pick some roses.'

On the way into his bedroom, Ben trod on the floorboard and it squeaked at him. He threw his homework down on the little table that served as a desk and waited, looking out of the window, till he saw his mother go down the garden with a basket and a pair of secateurs. Then it was out with the Swiss Army knife, up with the floorboard and, once he'd replaced it, back into his room with the canvas bag. Breathless with excitement, he loosened the drawstring and tipped the coins out on to the table.

They were all exactly the same, all gold, and there were twenty-five of them.

A glance out of the window showed him that his mother was still busy, so he took a careful look at one of the coins.

On one side of it was a picture of a man's head, looking from left to right. He looked like a fat man from his double chins, and he had pop eyes, a big curved nose and long wavy hair down to his shoulders.

Round the rim of that side of the gold coin
was written

GEORGIUS III DEI GRATIA.

Ben didn't know what the last two words
meant, but he could tell that this was a coin
from the reign of King George the Third,
whenever that might have been.

He turned it over.

On the other side was a shield shaped like a
spade, not the ordinary squarish spade but one
with a point to its blade. Round this rim was
written

M.B.F.ET.H.REX.F.D.B.ET.L.D.S.R.I.A.T.ET.E.

And then a date: 1787.

'Wow!' said Ben. 'It's really old!'

He had no idea what all those letters meant
but the date was plain enough. He looked
through all the others. They were all exactly
the same except that they had different dates,
ranging from 1787 to 1799.

He looked out in the garden. His mother
was no longer there. Then he heard her foot-
steps, coming upstairs.

There was a drawer in the table, and Ben opened it, swept into it the bag and all the coins, closed it, and then grabbed his maths exercise book and a pen. He sat very close to the table, his tummy against the drawer.

His mother looked round the door.

'What was that crashing noise I just heard?' she asked.

'Just counting my money, Mum,' said Ben.

'You and your money! It sounded like an awful lot. How much have you got altogether now?'

'I don't know,' said Ben.

Yet, he thought. What are these gold coins worth? How shall I find out?

His mother came into the room and looked over Ben's shoulder.

'Maths homework?' she said.

'Yes.'

'What a mess your table is in. And I expect that drawer is too. What's in it?'

'Only my money,' said Ben truthfully.

'Your precious cash-box, you mean?'

'Yes,' said Ben, truthfully again.

And twenty-five gold coins, he thought, but you don't know that, Mum, and I'm not going to tell you, and if you ask to look in the

drawer, I shall say – no, you can't, it's my drawer in my table in my bedroom so it's private.

Thinking all this made him go quite red in the face.

'Don't get yourself in a state,' his mother said. 'I'm not going to ask to look in your old drawer. Just tidy things up a bit, will you, please?' And she went out of the room.

Ben waited until he could hear small hammering noises downstairs which meant, he knew, that his mother was busy bashing the ends of the stems of the roses she'd cut before arranging them in water. Then he opened the drawer, and counted the twenty-five gold coins carefully back into the bag and drew the drawstring tight.

I think I'll just leave it in here, he thought. Mum said she wouldn't look in this drawer and Dad never comes into my room. It'd be safer under the floorboard, I suppose – after all, it's been safe there for around two hundred years – but if I keep it here just for now I can take one with me to school tomorrow and try and find a book in the library that will tell me what sort of coin it is.

Later that evening, as Ben was saying goodnight before going up to bed, his father said, 'Watch out as you go along the landing.'

'Why?' said Ben.

'I've been doing a bit of DIY. Mum said there's a floorboard outside your bedroom that's been squeaking worse than usual, so I've fixed it. I've put some good long countersunk screws in it to keep it rigid. It won't move again in a hurry. And I've given it a coat of stain which will still be wet, so mind where you put your feet.'

'Oh,' said Ben.

'I had a peep in your room too.'

'Oh,' said Ben.

'Glad to see you've tidied your table up,' said his father. 'Mum said it was in an awful mess. The only thing that puzzled me was that

I couldn't see that cash-box of yours. Then I had a look in the drawer and there it was.'

'Oh,' said Ben.

'And I noticed you had an old bag in there that was full of money by the feel of it. I didn't open it of course, but it weighed heavy. Where did you get all that lot?'

CHAPTER 3

YELLOW PAGES

What shall I say? thought Ben.

Tell a lie? Say it's just a lot of 2p pieces? No.

Make a joke? Say it fell off the back of a lorry? No.

'Oh, those are just some old coins that I collected,' he said truthfully.

'What are you going to do with all this money you've got, Ben?' his mother said. 'Is there something special you're saving for?'

'I haven't decided,' said Ben. 'Yet.'

I don't know what the gold coins are worth, he thought. Yet, I might be as rich as old . . . what was his name? . . . oh yes, Croesus, that's it.

In the morning Ben decided against taking

one of his coins to school. Instead he took one from the bag, made a careful drawing of each side of it, and put it back.

At morning break it was raining, so the children were not allowed out into the playground but stayed in their classrooms. Ben asked if he could go to the library. After a lot of searching, he found a book about coins, and in it, under 'George III', was the picture he wanted, identical, he could see, with the drawing which he had made.

There was the fat old double-chinned king on the obverse side, and on the reverse, all those letters and a date – 1787, just like his oldest coin. Underneath the picture, it said

> George III spade guinea, so called because the medallion on the reverse side resembles the 'spade' on a playing card. Between 1787 and 1799, more of these gold coins were struck than any other coin of this reign.

What's a guinea worth? Ben thought. He looked in a dictionary.

> Guinea. An obsolete English gold coin, first made of gold brought from Guinea

in Africa. Its value finally, one pound, one shilling.

Like many people who are interested in money, Ben was good at maths. 5p, he knew, was the same as an old shilling, and there had been twenty shillings to the pound. So one pound, one shilling – a guinea – was 105p. And he had twenty-five of them. And twenty-five times 105 was – he worked out the sum on the back of the drawing of the coin – £26.25.

Not exactly a fortune.

But surely guineas as old as that, round about two hundred years old, must be worth more now. How much more? How could he find out? The answer to that came, quite by chance, that very evening.

'Something's gone wrong with the hot tap in the bath,' his mother told his father. 'Even when it's turned on full, it still only gives out a trickle of water. It's bunged up somehow.'

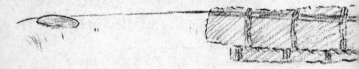

'I'll have a look,' Ben's father said, but when he had, he said, 'It's beyond me, I'm afraid. There's a sort of widget in it that seems to be bust. It's a job for a plumber.'

'Do we know one?' Ben's mother said.

'No. Better have a look in the Yellow Pages.'

That's it! thought Ben. And later, when his parents were watching TV, he looked in the index of the Yellow Pages and found

COIN AND MEDAL DEALERS, p. 316.

There were only two names under this heading, both local numbers. Ben took a penny out of his pocket.

'Heads it's the Curio Shop,' he said, 'and tails it's H. J. Garter.'

The penny came down tails.

First making sure his mother and father were still glued to the television, Ben picked up the cordless phone that had been left in the kitchen and dialled the second number.

'Hullo,' said a voice. 'Harry Garter speaking.'

'Please,' said Ben, 'can you tell me the value of an old gold coin? We've got a book on coins in our school library, but it doesn't tell you how much different coins are worth.'

'I see,' said Harry Garter. 'You're doing a project, I expect. What coin is it that you want to know about?'

'A George III spade guinea.'

'Ah yes, there are quite a lot of those about. They're not worth a great deal.'

'Oh dear,' said Ben.

'Mind you,' said Harry Garter, 'from a collector's point of view they are still worth having. Better than a poke in the eye with a blunt stick. And for somebody your age for example – how old are you, might I ask?'

'Eight.'

'Just so. Somebody your age might be quite glad to sell me a spade guinea.'

'Suppose I had one,' said Ben. 'How much would you give me?'

'For one?'

'Yes.'

'Like I said, not a lot,' replied Harry Garter. 'I'm afraid I shouldn't be able to offer you more than £80.'

CHAPTER 4

TREASURE TROVE

'£80?' said Ben.

'Yes.'

'For one spade guinea?'

'Yes,' said Harry Garter. 'Look, if you're interested, I could show you one. It might help you with your project. Where do you live?'

Ben told him.

'Well, that's no distance – I have an office on the ground floor of my house – 99 High Street. I carry on my business from home. I'm semi-retired, you know, got grandchildren about your age. I'd be happy to show you my collection of coins. Look in next time you're passing.'

'Thanks,' said Ben.

'What's your name, by the way?' asked Harry Garter, but Ben, hearing his mother's voice, had put the phone down.

Later, he did more sums. £80 each! And he had twenty-five of them. That meant that altogether they were worth . . . £2,000! All he had to do was take the bag of guineas to this Mr Garter – and he walked along the High Street every day on his way to and from school, right past the door of Number 99!

On the other hand, thought Ben, I don't know anything about this old chap. He sounded nice on the phone, but they're always telling us at school not to accept sweets from strangers and stuff like that. Why does he want to show me his coins? He might be a child murderer or something, I'd better not go on my own. I know! I'll get Jamie to come with me.

Jamie was Ben's best friend at school, and lived just along the road, so that they always walked to and from school together.

Before he went to bed that night, Ben put a sticky label on the front of the drawer in his desk. It said

STRICKTLY PRIVATE

Before he went to school next morning he left on top of his desk an envelope, also marked

STRICKTLY PRIVATE

Under these two words was written

NOT TO BE OPENED UNLESS I DONT COME BACK FROM SCHOOL TODAY.

Inside the envelope was a sheet of paper with this message

IF I DO NOT RETURN, GET THE POLLICE TO GO TO 99 HIGH STREET AND AREST HARRY GARTER THE CHILD MURDERER AND TELL JAMIE'S MUM I'M SORRY HE GOT MURDERED TOO.

At school, in the morning break, he said to Jamie, 'I've got to see a man on the way home from school this afternoon. He's a coin man. He's going to show me some coins. D'you want to see them too?'

Jamie was a boy of few words. He never used two if one would do, and he did not use one unless it was absolutely necessary. Now he nodded.

'You're not in a hurry to get home from school, are you?' Ben said.

Jamie shook his head.

'It's at Number 99 in the High Street. You'll come in with me then will you?'

There was a time when Jamie might have replied, 'OK,' but he had managed to shorten this.

'K,' he said.

So, not long after half past three, the two boys stood outside Number 99. There was a bell beside the front door with a card by it saying

H. GARTER. RING FOR ADMITTANCE

Ben pressed it.

In a couple of seconds a voice that seemed to come from somewhere just beside the bell said, 'Who is it?'

'Ben,' said Ben.

'I don't know any Bens,' said the voice.

'I rang you up. About the spade guinea.'

'Oh yes, I remember,' said the voice, and there was a clicking noise.

'Come on in. Just push the door, it will open now.'

Inside, the boys found themselves in a hall-way, and then a door at the end opened and there stood the figure of a large old man with a lot of silvery hair and a round red smiling face.

'Hullo,' he said. 'I'm Harry Garter. Which of you is Ben?'

'I am,' said Ben.

He doesn't *look* like a child murderer, he thought as the old man shook his hand.

'Is it all right for us to have a look at your coins?' he said. 'I've brought my friend Jamie.'

'Of course,' said Harry Garter. 'How do you do, Jamie?'

''lo,' said Jamie.

'Come into my office,' said the coin dealer, opening a door at the side of the hall. 'This is where I keep my collection. By the way, I hope you're not burglars, are you? You don't *look* like burglars.'

Ben, grinning, said, 'No, we're not burglars.'

Jamie shook his head.

'Because the stuff in here's worth a great deal, that's why I have that security gadget on the front door. I hope you're not burglars' sons either?'

'My dad's an auctioneer,' said Ben. 'Tell him what yours is, Jamie.'

'Vet,' said Jamie.

'That's nice and short,' said Harry Garter. 'Now a coin collector's got a very long name. My eldest grandson has only just learned to spell it. Numismatologist.'

'Wow!' said Ben. 'I couldn't even say that, let alone spell it, could you, Jamie?'

'No,' said Jamie.

'Now then,' said Harry Garter, smiling, 'have a look at some of these.'

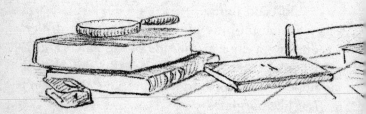

From a cabinet in the corner of the room he brought out a number of trays. In them were coins of many different sizes and of several different metals, copper, bronze, silver and gold.

Some had lovely names – stour royal, rose noble, half-thistle, Briton crown, George noble and double-eagle. There were two among them that caught Ben's eye, one placed to show King George III's head, one to show the shield on the reverse side, shaped like the symbol for a spade in a pack of cards. He pointed at them.

'Yes,' said Harry Garter. 'Those are the spade guineas you were inquiring about. They were all minted between 1787 and 1799, in the reign of George III. Why did you particularly want to know about spade guineas, Ben?'

Ben thought fast.

'I saw a picture of them in a book, in the library at school,' he said. 'And I sort of made up a story about them.'

'How did it go?'

'Well, you see, there was this boy and he lived in an old house and he found a bag full of gold coins under the floorboards.'

'Aha!' said Harry Garter. 'Treasure Trove!'

'What does that mean?' asked Ben.

'Anyone who finds gold, or silver, has to report it to the police and they in turn report it to a person called the Coroner. Treasure Trove, you see, is rightly the property of the Crown. It belongs to the Queen, not to the finder.'

CHAPTER 5

---

99 HIGH STREET

School ended at 3.30 and usually Ben was home before four o'clock, after he and Jamie had dawdled along the High Street, looking in shop windows and chattering to one another (at least Ben chattered while Jamie grunted monosyllabic replies).

But that day 4.30 came with no sign of Ben and his mother became worried. Because the distance from school was short and the High Street always full of people, because there were no roads to cross except by zebra crossings, and because they both considered their sons were now old enough to act sensibly, Ben's mother and Jamie's mother – who were also friends – had decided that the boys could make their own way to and from school. If the weather was vile, one or other mother would drive them there or fetch them.

Sometimes there were Clubs after the end of school – Chess Club, Gym Club or Football – but Ben didn't say anything about today, his mother thought. Would he have left a note on his desk perhaps?

She hurried upstairs and found the envelope saying

STRICKTLY PRIVATE
NOT TO BE OPENED UNLESS I DONT COME
BACK FROM SCHOOL TODAY

She tore it open. Then she hurried to the phone and dialled a number.

'Susan,' she said, 'it's Helen. Is Jamie home?'

'No,' said Jamie's mother. 'I was just going to ring you. Isn't Ben either?'

'No, but look, don't worry, he's left me a note, with an address. I can't explain now because I don't know what they're up to, but I'll find out straight away and ring you back.'

Child murderer! she thought. Stupid boy! But all the same she gave a shiver.

Quickly she looked up 'Garter' in the phone book. There was only one, at 99 High Street. She dialled the number.

'Hullo,' said a man's voice.

'Oh, hullo,' said Ben's mother. 'Mr Garter?'

'Speaking.'

'My name is Helen Bishop. My son Ben left me a note giving your address. Is he with you?'

'He was,' said Harry Garter.

'Was?' said Ben's mother in a voice that broke a little. Child murderer, she thought. Don't be so stupid, she thought.

'Yes. He's just left. With his friend.'

'Called Jamie?'

'Yes.'

'Oh.'

'You sound upset, Mrs Bishop,' said Harry Garter. 'There's no need, I assure you. I am a coin dealer and collector, and the boys were interested – something to do with a school project, I believe. They knocked on my door and I showed them my collection. Oh, and gave them some of my wife's rather rich chocolate cake. Other than that, they are quite unharmed.'

'Oh, I see,' said Ben's mother, embarrassed now at her suspicions of this pleasant-voiced kindly-seeming giver-out of chocolate cake. 'I'm sorry to have bothered you, Mr Garter.'

'I'm sorry to have worried you, Mrs Bishop.'

As she put the phone down, Ben's mother heard him coming in the front door. Like any mother who has had a fright, she pitched into him.

'Do you realize,' she said, 'that it's a quarter to five? Where have you been? I've been out of my mind with worry!'

'I left you a note, Mum,' Ben said. 'Didn't you see it?'

'I should think I did! I suppose you think that comforted me? I'm only glad that Jamie's mother didn't read it.'

'Oh, that was just a joke, Mum,' said Ben. 'This Mr Garter, he's a coin man, a newmisma-something or other, I can't say it, and he showed us his collection. It was jolly interesting. And he gave us some yummy chocolate cake.'

'I don't care about any of that,' said his mother. 'The fact is that you went into a perfectly strange house to see a perfectly strange man, and both Susan Parry and I have been worried stiff, and I shall tell your father the moment he gets home.'

Then she rang Jamie's mother.

'Is he home?' she said.

'Yes, I've just torn him off a strip.'

'It was Ben's fault.'

'At least he left you a note. Jamie hadn't said anything to me. Not that he ever does say much. But his father will have something to say to him.'

CHAPTER 6

J.E.F.

Walking to school next morning, Ben said to Jamie, 'My dad didn't half give me a rollicking last night. All about not speaking to strangers and that. I told him, Mr Garter's really nice, but he just said I was never to go there again. Did your dad bawl you out too?'

'Uh-huh,' said Jamie.

This, Ben knew, meant 'Yes'. 'No', in Jamie-speak, was 'Uh-uh'.

'I'm sorry,' he said. 'I got you into trouble, asking you to come with me.'

''S all right,' said Jamie.

On the way back from school that afternoon Ben paused for a moment as they passed Number 99. He was hoping that by chance

Harry Garter might come out of his front door, and then he could talk to him. He'd only been told not to go in, that's all. He could still talk to the man if he met him, surely. But no one came out, so they walked on.

At the end of the High Street stood the church, and sometimes the two boys would walk around the chuchyard before continuing towards home. A number of the gravestones were quite old, and Ben and Jamie had an ongoing competition to see who could find the oldest. The date that the person had been born was what they looked for, and Jamie held the record – 1807.

On this afternoon they hunted around for a bit, and then, in a far corner, under a spreading yew tree, Ben noticed an empty Coke can that someone had chucked away. One of those things they were keen on at school was that you shouldn't drop rubbish all over the place,

and that you should, when you found any, pick it up and put it in a bin.

Ben went to pick up the Coke can, and as he did so, he noticed a smallish gravestone he hadn't seen before, partly hidden as it was beneath the yew. Like many of the old stones, it was no longer upright, and this one leaned over at such an angle that Ben had to lie on his back on the grass to read what was written on it.

At first he could not make it out, so weathered and worn and moss-covered was the lettering, but once he had scraped away at it with his Swiss Army knife, he could read

HERE LIES

JACOB EBENEZER FAIRY

BORN THE FIFTH DAY OF MARCH 1750

DIED THE THIRD DAY OF JUNE 1802

'Jamie!' yelled Ben.

'What?'

'Look at this! Born 1750, this old guy was. That's the record, by a mile!'

'Uh-huh,' said Jamie.

Ben was home just after four o'clock.

His mother looked at her watch.

'That's better,' she said, 'though you're still a bit later than usual.'

'We were playing the gravestone game, Mum,' said Ben, 'and what d'you think? I found a man who was born in 1750!'

'This town would only have been a little village then,' his mother said. 'Just the church and the Manor House and a few old cottages.'

'Like ours?'

'Yes.'

Later that evening something very strange happened. Ben's parents were fairly strict about the television and didn't let him watch everything and anything all the time. Now it was off, and while his mother and father were talking, Ben sat on a stool by the fire, watching the dancing flames of the burning logs and wishing that his parents weren't so strict. He had rammed the poker into the heart of the fire to heat the tip of it so that he could burn holes in an unused log. Someone – a boy, he supposed, no, more like several different boys over the years – had once upon a time done that on the face of the great oak beam that was set into the wall above the fireplace and ran almost the width of the room.

There were a number of round black holes

an inch or so deep in the beam, and also some
initials burned into the wood. There was an A
at one end of the beam, and an M in the
middle, and at the other end someone had
burned all three of his initials.

J.E.F.

Ben had seen these three initials, black against
the tawny wood, hundreds of times without
ever thinking anything about them, but now,
suddenly, he saw them through different eyes.

Jacob Ebenezer Fairy! he said to himself. It
could be, he could have lived here! This cottage was built in the middle of the seventeenth
century, round about 1650, Dad told me. So
J.E.F. could easily have been born here, in
1750!

And if he was, the spade guineas could have been his life savings. Let's see — those coins were all minted between 1787 and 1799, so he started saving when he was — um — thirty-seven, and then when he died, suddenly perhaps, aged — um — fifty-two, he'd never used the money that he'd hidden for his old age.

That must be it! Jacob Ebenezer Fairy lived in this house and burned his initials into that beam when he was a boy. The gold had belonged to him, Fairy gold! And now it ought to belong to me, Ben thought, but because of this Treasure Trove business, it belongs to the old Queen. It's not fair, she didn't find it, I did.

'Take that poker out of the fire, Ben!' said his father. 'How many times do I have to tell you not to mess about like that. Look at it! It's red hot!'

'Sorry, Dad,' said Ben though he wasn't. 'By the way, it's Friday night.'

'So?'

'Pocket-money. And your small change for this week, please.'

A good week, he found when he'd counted it up. The usual £1 plus 93p in fives, twos and ones. Almost two pounds altogether. Yet upstairs in that bag in his desk was £2,000 worth of spade guineas.

Report it to the police, Mr Garter said you had to.

Blowed if I will.

CHAPTER 7

A SECRET

For some days Ben hung about for a little, each time they passed the door of Number 99 High Street, while Jamie waited patiently, silent as usual. That was what made him such a restful sort of friend, Ben thought, you didn't have to bother to explain things to him. He had considered letting Jamie in on his secret but had decided against it; not that Jamie would have told anyone else, he never told anyone anything else much, it would have meant too much talking. It was just that the more Ben thought about his bag of gold, the more he felt he wanted to keep it to himself – the gold and the secret.

I suppose I'm a miser, he said to himself,

and, not being quite sure what the word meant, he went to the school library next day and looked it up in a dictionary.

Miser. One who lives miserably in order to hoard wealth.

No, that's not right, he thought, I'm not miserable and I don't want to hoard the spade guineas, I want to sell them to Mr Garter, which is why I shall somehow have to meet him again to ask him more about this Treasure

Trove business. Perhaps there's some way out of putting it in the Queen's pocket; she's got bags of lolly already.

Then, perhaps because he'd just used a dictionary to find something out, he took down an encyclopedia. Maybe it would say something about Treasure Trove. It did!

> Treasure Trove is the property of the Crown and the finder of gold or silver must report it to the Coroner, via the police.

Yes, that's what Mr Garter had said. He read on.

> The gold or silver must have been hidden deliberately, with the intention of retrieving it later.

Well, it was, wasn't it? Mr Fairy must have meant to retrieve it later to make his old age – which he never reached – more comfortable. (Though maybe *he* was a miser, living miserably, hoarding his Fairy gold.) Ben read more.

> If the find is declared Treasure Trove and the original owner cannot be traced, then the finder can keep or sell it.

'Yeeow!' yelled Ben, punching the air, and a passing teacher said sharply, 'Stop that noise, Ben! You are meant to be quiet in the library, not making enough noise to wake the dead.'

I can't wake old Jacob Ebenezer anyway, thought Ben. He's been sleeping under the yew tree for nearly two hundred years, and no one but me knows that the gold was his. So I *can* sell it! To Mr Garter. For £2,000. But Dad said I was never to go to his house again.

Nothing to stop me ringing him up though, is there? I'll pretend I'm ringing Jamie.

As they walked home together Ben said, 'I'm going to pretend to ring you up this evening, Jamie.'

'Pretend?'

'Yes. You see, I want to use the phone to ring Mr Garter. I'll tell you why, one of these days.'

'K,' said Jamie.

'But I don't want Mum and Dad to know I'm ringing him. I mean, I'm going to tell them too but not yet. So I'm going to say I'm ringing you.'

'Uh-huh,' said Jamie.

'You don't mind if I don't tell you what it's all about yet?'

'Uh-uh.'

So that evening Ben asked if he could make a phone call.

'Who d'you want to ring?' his mother said.

'Jamie.'

'What about?'

'Some homework. I'm not sure what we've got to do. I need to ask him some questions.'

'Let's hope they don't need long answers,' Ben's father said. 'I don't think I've ever heard

Jamie put more than two words together.'

Ben had already looked up 'H. J. Garter' again in the directory and made a note of the number. Now, in another room, with the door shut, he hastily dialled it.

'Hullo,' said Harry Garter.

'Look, Mr Garter, it's Ben Bishop speaking, you know, you showed us your coins, and I'm sorry to bother you but I need to talk to you,' said Ben all in a rush.

'Talk away, Ben, talk away.'

'Well, I can't really now,' said Ben, 'because I'm supposed to be ringing up Jamie, not you, and Dad says I can't come to your house but perhaps we could meet somewhere and then I can tell you more.'

'Well, all right, Ben. Where shall we meet?'

'In the churchyard,' said Ben. 'Tomorrow at four o'clock. If you can manage that?'

The door opened and Ben's father came in.

'Thanks, Jamie,' said Ben hurriedly. 'I wasn't sure if we had to do all the sums on page 30. See you tomorrow,' and he rang off.

As they reached the churchyard on their way home the following afternoon, Ben said to his friend, 'Let's play our usual game, shall we?'

'K,' said Jamie.

But, search as they might, neither could find a date of birth earlier than 1750. Ben consulted his watch. It said a quarter to four.

'You get on home if you like,' he said to Jamie. 'I'm going to stop here a bit and find some dandelions for my rabbit. You might just knock on our door as you go past and tell my mum that's what I'm doing, will you?'

'K,' said Jamie.

Once he had gone, Ben did pick a few dandelions, and then he sat on top of a big coffin-shaped gravestone, under which, so the message read, lay Colonel Sir Brandon Fairbrother, who had departed this life in 1890, and his dearly beloved wife Laetitia, who had made it to the end of the century.

Before long Ben saw the large silver-haired figure of the coin dealer coming through the churchyard gates, and, leaving the dandelions on top of the coffin, he jumped down and ran to meet him.

'Thanks for coming,' he said.

'That's all right,' said Harry Garter. 'No distance. Now what's all this about? I smell a mystery. Tell me.'

So Ben told him – how he'd found the gold,

and how, thanks to the gravestone game and to the initials burned into the sitting-room beam, he was certain that the coins had once belonged to Jacob Ebenezer Fairy.

'Look, his gravestone's just over there,' he said. 'Under that yew tree. I'll show you.'

And, rather to Ben's surprise, Mr Garter, although old and heavy, lay down on the grass so that he too could read the inscription on the leaning stone. When he had levered himself to his feet again, he said, 'So that's why you wanted to know the value of a spade guinea. Nothing to do with a school project, or some story you were supposed to be writing – *you* were the boy who found the gold coins under the floorboards.'

'Yes. Twenty-five of them.'

Harry Garter gave a long low whistle.

'Twenty-five spade guineas?' he said.

'Yes. You said one was worth £80, so that adds up to £2,000 for the lot. And I looked up all about Treasure Trove in an encyclopaedia and it said that the finder could keep it and sell it if the original owner couldn't be traced.'

Harry Garter's round red face broke into a smile, and then he laughed out loud.

'Yes, but it sounds as though you've traced

him, Ben,' he said, resting one hand upon the leaning gravestone.

'Yes, but nobody knows that except you and me.'

'A secret, eh? All right, but I don't think it would make much odds if they did. Mr Fairy's gold's no use to him. Mind you, I must tell you straight away, Ben, that just because I quoted you £80 for one spade guinea, that doesn't necessarily mean that I can offer you £2,000 for twenty-five of them. I might have difficulty finding a customer. And a lot depends on their condition. I shan't know till I see them. Which brings me on to the next thing. You say that you've told your parents nothing of all this?'

'No.'

'Told Jamie?'

'No. Only you.'

'And you want my help?'

'Yes. Please.'

'Right. Now then, I don't mind keeping Mr Fairy a secret but everything else has got to come out into the open. Your parents have got to be told, and then, if they're agreeable, I can help with the business of reporting the find to the proper authorities. And once it's declared Treasure Trove, then you can think about selling and I can think about buying. Understand?'

'Yes.'

'It should all be quite straightforward,' said Harry Garter with another pat on the leaning gravestone, 'precisely because it will not be possible to trace the original owner of the gold.' They stepped out from under the shadow of the yew tree and walked together to the churchyard gate. Then the coin dealer stuck out his large old hand. Ben shook it.

'Thanks,' he said. 'Thanks a lot.'

'Don't thank me,' said Harry Garter. 'Thank Mr Fairy. And your lucky stars,' and he turned to walk back up the High Street.

Ben set off home, running, and soon could see his mother standing by their garden gate. 'Sorry I'm late,' he called. 'Did Jamie tell you? I was collecting some . . .' and then he stopped, remembering that they were still lying

72

on top of Colonel Sir Brandon and Lady Fairbrother.

'. . . dandelions,' finished his mother. 'So I see. Or rather so I don't see. What exactly have you been up to, Ben?'

'Can we wait till Dad gets home, Mum?' Ben said. 'Then I can tell you both.'

And that evening he told them the whole story from the beginning, and then brought down the old canvas bag from the drawer in his table, and undid the drawstring, and tipped out the shower of gleaming, gold coins.

'Why on earth haven't you told us about this before, Ben?' his father said. 'It would have been more honest.'

Ben couldn't think what to say to this, and fell into Jamie-speak.

'Dunno,' he said.

'Secrets aren't good in a family,' his mother said. 'But anyway, we won't say any more about that. Now then, you say these are spade guineas?'

'Yes. George III. Twenty-five of them.'

'Worth £80 each?' asked his father. 'That's . . . let's see . . . £2,000.'

'Yes. If I'm allowed to sell them. And if Mr Garter offers me that much.'

'How exciting!' they said.

'You lucky boy!' said his mother.

'You rich boy!' said his father. 'Almost as rich as Croesus.'

'And I've got £15.50 in my cash-box,' said Ben.

'You won't be needing my small change on top of your pocket-money any more, then?'

'Oh yes, I will!'

Next morning there was the usual single knock on the Bishops' front door, which meant that Jamie Parry was outside, waiting to walk to school with Ben. Ben's father had already left for work, having rung Mr Garter and arranged to leave the bag of gold with him so that the business of proving Treasure Trove could begin.

'By the way,' said Ben as the two boys set off, 'I can tell you now.'

'What?' said Jamie.

'What I couldn't tell you before because it was a secret. You know, all about Mr Garter and that. You see, I found something, in our house, under the floor.'

He paused, but Jamie plodded on without speaking, so he said, 'Go on. Ask me what it was.'

'K,' said Jamie. 'What?'

'Gold coins. A bag full of gold coins. Golden guineas. Twenty-five of them!'

Jamie stopped, and turned and looked directly at Ben.

That shook him! Ben thought. He may not be the world's most talkative guy but I bet he'll have a lot to say about that!

He waited, but Jamie didn't speak, though a broad smile spread over his face.

'Well?' said Ben. 'Aren't you pleased for me?'

Jamie nodded his head, several times.

'Uh-huh,' he said. 'Uh-huh.'

CHAPTER 8

FAIRY GOLD

For a couple of weeks Ben heard nothing further about the Fairy gold. 'Has Mr Garter rung up?' was his first question on arriving home from school, and the answer was always, 'No. Not yet.'

But then there came a morning when Ben's father received an official letter from the Coroner's Office.

Reading it, he learned that the gold found in his house and submitted for the Coroner's inspection by Mr H. J. Garter of 99 High Street had, in the absence of any other claimant, been declared Treasure Trove, and so could be kept or sold by the finder.

He passed the letter across to his wife.

'Oh!' she said. 'How wonderful!' and they both looked at Ben, who was eating fish fingers.

'How many?' his mother had asked before breakfast, and he had replied, 'A handful, please.' This was a Ben joke. When asked what a handful meant, he would answer, 'Four fish fingers and a fish thumb.'

They watched him shovelling them in.

'Nice?' his mother said.

'Mmm.'

'Here's something else nice too,' his father said. 'From the Coroner's Office. You are allowed to sell your gold coins.'

'Yeeow!' cried Ben through a mouthful of fish finger.

'A copy of this has gone to Mr Garter, it says, so we'll probably be hearing from him soon. And now I must be off. I've got a big farm sale the other side of the county, so I'll probably be late back.'

And indeed he was, for at the sale a cattle-lorry backed into his Range Rover and caused, so the garageman that towed him in estimated, £2,000 worth of damage.

When Ben arrived home from school, his mother told him what had happened.

'Dad's quite all right,' she said. 'He wasn't in the car – it was parked when the wretched lorry hit it.'

'Did it do a lot of damage?' Ben asked.

'About £2,000 worth, apparently,' said his mother. It did not occur to her that this was a sum of money that had been in Ben's thoughts for quite some time. Now he began to think along quite different lines.

Suppose Mr Garter does give me £2,000 for my spade guineas? He might, he didn't say he wouldn't. Perhaps I ought to give it to Dad to get the Range Rover mended.

Next day, walking to school, he said to Jamie, 'Our car got busted yesterday. It got hit by a cattle-lorry.'

At this, Jamie made quite a long speech.

'Hope your dad wasn't hurt,' he said.

'No, he wasn't in it.'

They walked on a bit.

'You know that gold I found?' said Ben.

'Uh-huh.'

'Well, I'm allowed to sell it, and I'm going to give the money to Dad.'

'Why?'

'To mend the car.'

'Oh.'

'D'you think that's a good idea?'

'S'pose so.'

'Would you do it, if you were me?'

'Uh-uh,' said Jamie.

'What would you do with it, then?'

'Spend it.'

All through that school day Ben thought about this. Jamie was right of course. Nine hundred and ninety-nine boys out of a thousand would spend the money without a second thought, to buy computers, CD players, mountain bikes, all sorts of things.

But is it really my money to spend? Ben said to himself. I know I found the gold, but I found it in our house which is Dad's house so you could say it's Dad's gold. What shall I do?

As they walked down the High Street on their way home, who should they meet but Harry Garter, coming out of the supermarket with a carrier bag in each hand.

'Hullo, Ben! Hullo, Jamie!' he said, and Ben said, 'Hullo, Mr Garter,' and Jamie said, ''lo,' and Ben said, 'Excuse me, but will you be buying my spade guineas?' and Harry Garter said, 'I'm certainly interested in buying them, Ben, but I can't make you an offer yet. I'll tell you why. I have a client in America who I have to contact first. As soon as I hear back from him, I'll be in touch. You're pretty excited about it all, I expect. Made your mind up what you're going to do with the money?'

'No,' said Ben. 'Not yet.'

But when his father came home from work, in the car he'd hired while the Range Rover was being mended, Ben found that his mind was made up.

'Dad,' he said. 'Is that right – it's going to cost £2,000 to repair our car?'

'Yes.'

'Well, I saw Mr Garter in the High Street today and he said he's interested in buying my gold coins and if I get – I mean, if *we* get £2,000 for them, I think we should use that to put our car right. I mean, the spade guineas were hidden in our house – it's just that I happened to find them.'

Ben's father put his arms round his son and gave him a big hug.

'That's a very nice idea of yours, Ben,' he said, 'and I'm very grateful for the thought. But it's all right – the insurance company will pay the cost of the repairs. Whatever money the gold fetches is yours, to do what you want with. If I were you, I think I'd buy myself a nice present and then put the rest into a savings account. And don't be too sure about getting £2,000. Mr Garter might not offer you that much.'

'No, he told me that. But he might. He might even offer more, you never know your luck. Tell you what, Dad, I've just had an idea. If he gives me more than £2,000 – say, £2,100 perhaps – I'll give the extra to you, just like you give me your spare change.

Anything over £2,000 will be your pocket-money. Agreed?'

Ben's father laughed.

'We'll see,' he said. 'You may be interested in money, but you're still a generous chap, thank goodness. It says somewhere in the Bible that it's more blessed to give than to receive, and that's something we all ought to remember.'

Another week went by with no further word from the coin dealer. Then one day when Ben's mother and Jamie's mother were shopping together in the High Street, they were browsing through the brochures in a travel agents.

'Look at this, Susan,' said Helen Bishop. '"Two weeks in Majorca, self-catering, two adults, one child, flights included, £1,000." I'd love to go to Majorca. And as for Ben, it says there are masses of activities for children at this place, in something called the Happihols Sports Club.'

'Sounds good value, Helen,' said Susan Parry. 'What will Tom think about it?'

'Only one way to find out,' said Ben's mother, and she put the brochure in her shopping bag.

'Oh, I don't know, Helen,' said Tom Bishop that evening. 'It's a lot of money.'

'For two weeks? It's a bargain.'

'Well, we could always go to the seaside instead.'

'As usual. But I'd like to go to Majorca.'

'Majorca?' said Ben, pricking up his ears. 'Can we? Let's have a look.' And when he'd read the details, he said, 'This Sports Club sounds fab! Masses of things to do!'

'I don't know,' his father said again. 'Another time perhaps. What with the cost of repairing the Range Rover.'

'The insurance is paying for that, Dad, you said so,' said Ben.

'Yes, but still . . .'

There was a knock on the front door.

Ben went to open it and there stood Harry Garter.

'Hullo, Ben. Can I come in?' he said.

And when he'd shaken hands with the Bishops, he said, 'I'll get straight to the point, if I may. I've come to make Ben an offer for his twenty-five George III spade guineas. I think you were hoping to get £2,000, Ben?'

'Yes.'

'That's not what I can offer you.'

'No?'

'No. You see, thirteen of those twenty-five make up a complete set, one coin for each year of their mintage, from 1787 to 1799. The remaining twelve are duplicates, of various dates – those I can dispose at the market price. But the set of thirteen is much more valuable, something a wealthy American client of mine

has been on the lookout for for a long time. He is prepared to pay handsomely for them, which means that I find that, instead of offering you £2,000, Ben, I can now increase that offer to £3,000.'

'Yeeow!' yelled Ben, and then he turned to his father and said, 'The extra £1,000 is your pocket-money, remember? So now there's nothing to stop us going to Majorca.'

And then Ben and his father explained the 'pocket-money' bit of it to Ben's mother and the 'Majorca' bit of it to the coin dealer, and the whole lot of them were grinning like Cheshire cats.

'It's like a fairy story,' said Helen Bishop.

Harry Garter caught Ben's eye and then he shut one of his own quickly in a private wink.

'Funny you should say that,' he remarked. 'There's a name in the dictionary for "money that comes unsought". It's called "fairy gold".'